One of Those Days

words by
Amy Krouse Rosenthal

drawings by
Rebecca Doughty

G.P. Putnam's Sons

G. P. PUTNAM'S SONS

A division of Penguin Young Readers Group. Published by The Penguin Group.

Penguin Group (USA) Inc., 375 Hudson Street, New York, NY 10014, U.S.A.

Penguin Group (Canada), 90 Eglinton Avenue East, Suite 700, Toronto, Ontario, Canada M4P 2Y3

(a division of Pearson Penguin Canada Inc.).

Penguin Books Ltd, 80 Strand, London WC2R 0RL, England.

Penguin Ireland, 25 St. Stephen's Green, Dublin 2, Ireland (a division of Penguin Books Ltd.).

Penguin Group (Australia), 250 Camberwell Road, Camberwell, Victoria 3124, Australia

(a division of Pearson Australia Group Pty Ltd).

Penguin Books India Pvt Ltd, 11 Community Centre, Panchsheel Park, New Delhi - 110 017, India.

Penguin Group (NZ), Cnr Airborne and Rosedale Roads, Albany, Auckland 1310, New Zealand

(a division of Pearson New Zealand Ltd).

Penguin Books (South Africa) (Pty) Ltd, 24 Sturdee Avenue, Rosebank, Johannesburg 2196, South Africa.

Penguin Books Ltd, Registered Offices: 80 Strand, London WC2R 0RL, England.

Published simultaneously in Canada. Manufactured in China by South China Printing Co. Ltd.

Design by Marikka Tamura. Text set in ITC Goudy Sans Medium. The art was done in Flashe paint and ink on bristol board.

Library of Congress Cataloging-in-Publication Data

Rosenthal, Amy Krouse.

One of those days / words by Amy Krouse Rosenthal ; drawings by Rebecca Doughty. p. cm.

Summary: Children show that even when you have an unpleasant Sad for no Reason Day, an Itchy Sweater Day,

or an Annoying Sibling Day, you can expect a better day tomorrow. [1. Attitude (Psychology)—Fiction.]

I. Doughty, Rebecca, 1955–, ill. II. Title. PZ7.R719445One 2006 [E]—dc22 2005021882 ISBN 0-399-24365-8

1 3 5 7 9 10 8 6 4 2

First Impression

for Matt
  -AKR

for Ellen
  -RD

Some days are just not as great as others.
Some days are *one of those days*.

And the thing is, there isn't just one kind of
one of those days—there are tons. . . .

BUS
STOP

Annoying Sibling Day

Running Late Day

One Freak Hair Day

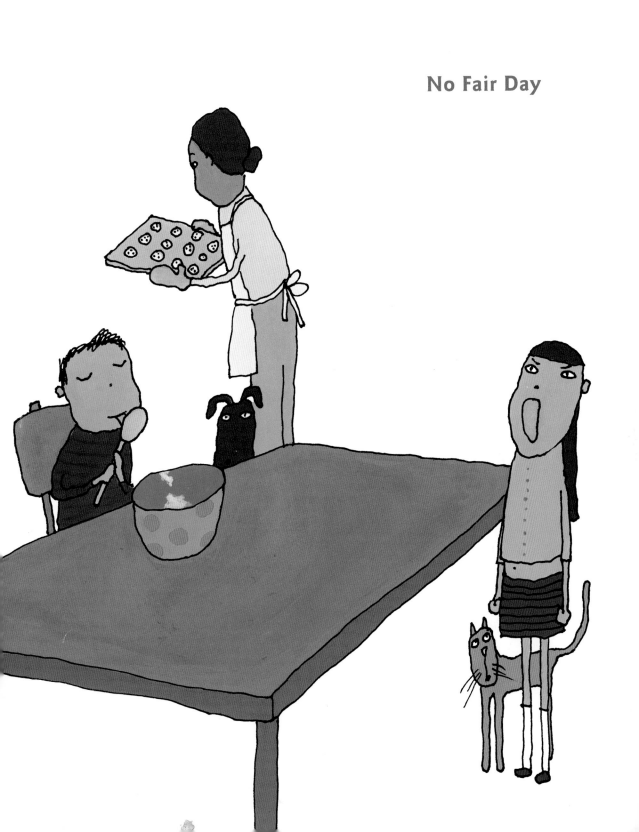

Favorite Pants Too Short Day

Keep Spilling Stuff Day

Nobody's Listening To You Day

Itchy Sweater Day

Too
Windy
Out
Day

Say The Wrong Thing Day

Best Friend Acting More Like
Your *Beast* Friend Day

Fun Thing Canceled Day

Big Day Kinda Disappointing Day

Gutter Ball Day

Can't Afford It Day

Feeling Left Out Day

Can't Find Stuff Day

Not Big Enough Day

Sad For No Reason Day

Luckily, every single *one of those days*
eventually turns into night.

And every single night turns into a brand-new day.